LIFEGUARD
ON
DUTY

# SEA REX

*by*

Molly Idle

VIKING
An Imprint of Penguin Group (USA)

*READY* for a carefree day of fun in the sun?
Gather your friends . . .

BEACH

. . . and head to the beach!

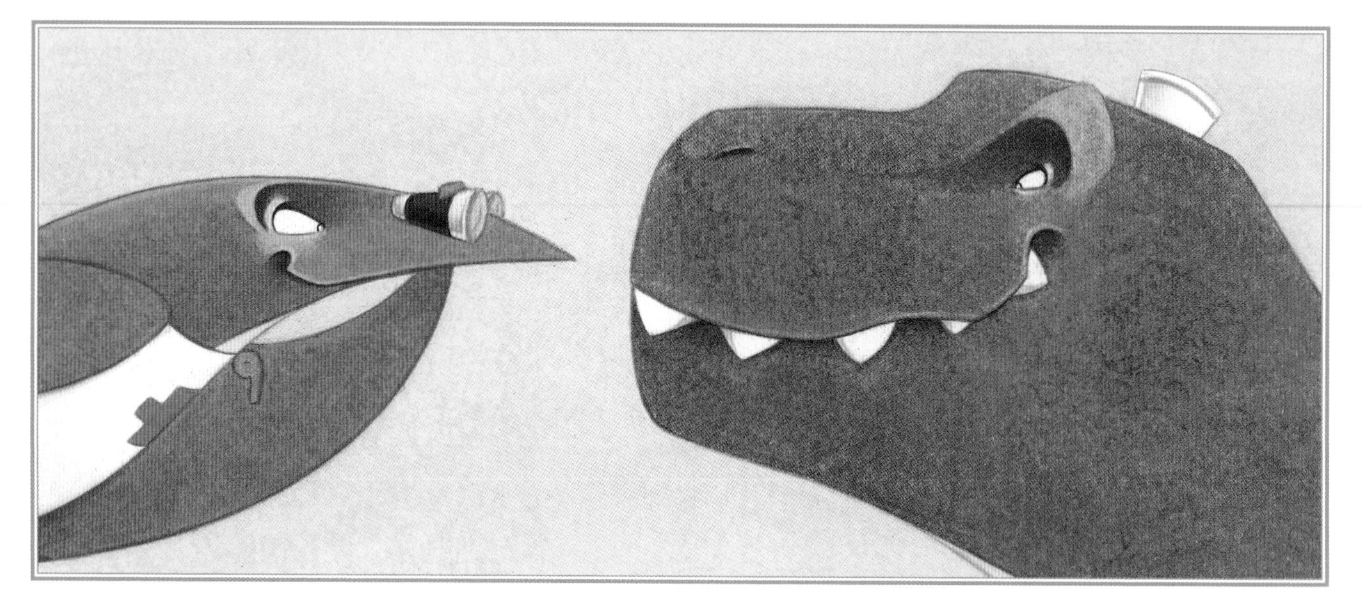

Station yourself near a lifeguard who will keep an eye on you.

Use plenty of sunscreen.

And remember, when testing the waters . . .

always jump in feet first.

If the surf is up, you can catch a few waves . . .

Or stay on land, and see what washes ashore.

You never know what treasures you may find.

Even the smallest shell . . .

. . . can contain the ocean's mighty roar!

Everyone loves a picnic at the beach,

so bring plenty to share.

But remember, you should wait to go in the water after eating.

And always swim with a buddy . . .

because you never know when the need for help might arise.

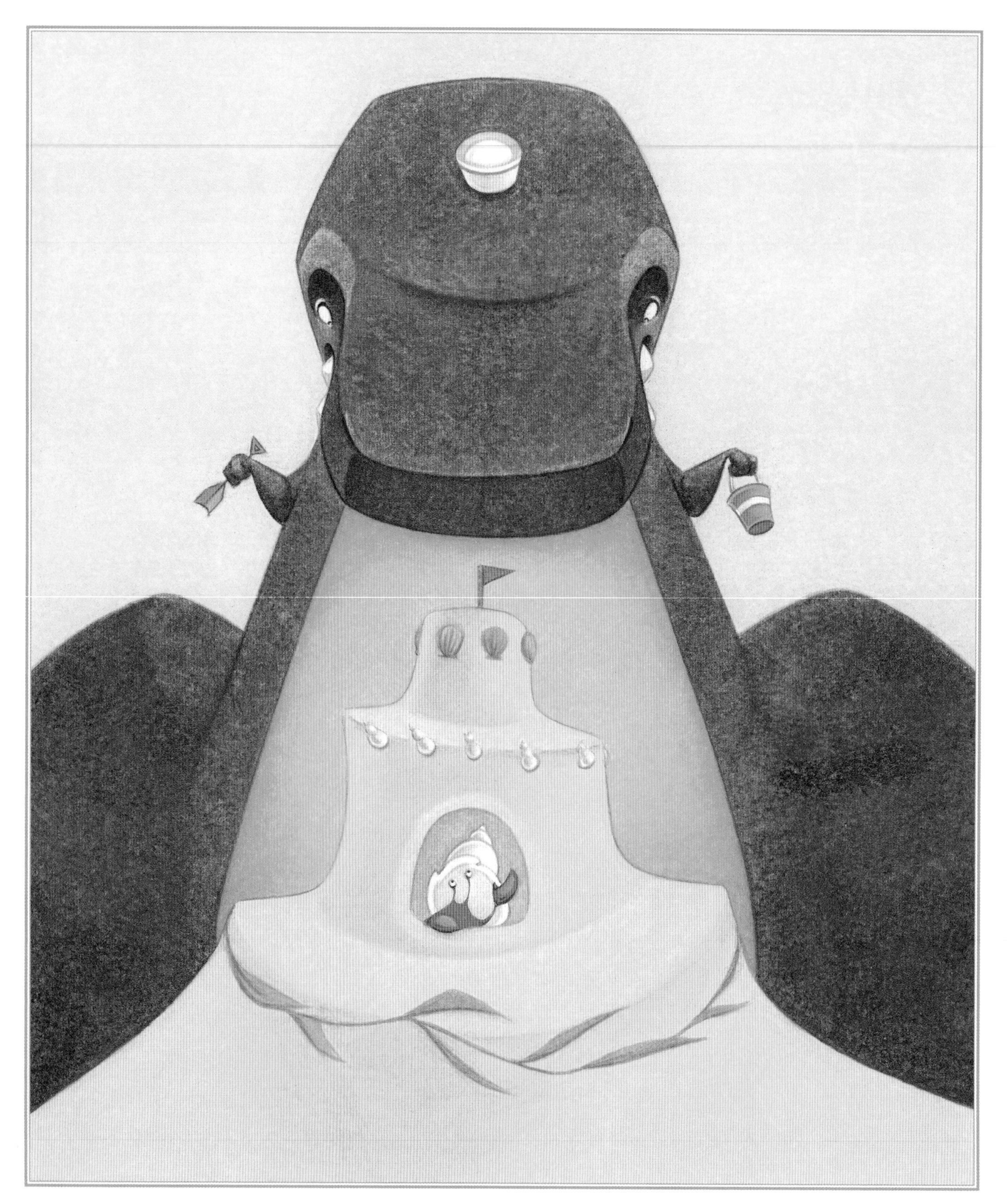

No matter how you choose to enjoy the sand, sea, and sun,
one thing is for sure . . .

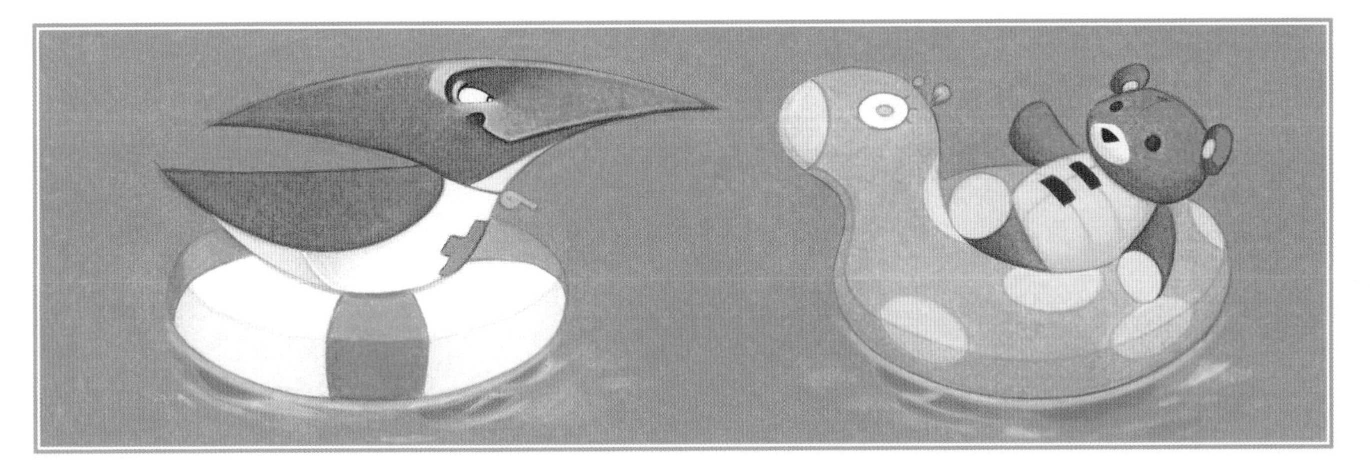

When you're surrounded
by friends . . .

life's a day at the beach.

*To Stevie D. by the Sea*

VIKING
Published by the Penguin Group
Penguin Group (USA) LLC
375 Hudson Street
New York, New York 10014

USA ✦ Canada ✦ UK ✦ Ireland ✦ Australia ✦ New Zealand ✦ India ✦ South Africa ✦ China
penguin.com
A Penguin Random House Company

First published in the United States of America by Viking, an imprint of Penguin Young Readers Group, 2015



LIBRARY OF CONGRESS CATALOGING-IN-PUBLICATION DATA
Idle, Molly Schaar, author.
Sea Rex / by Molly Idle.
pages cm
Summary: Cordelia spends a day at the beach with her dinosaur friends.
ISBN 978-0-670-78574-2
1. Tyrannosaurus rex—Juvenile fiction. 2. Dinosaurs—Juvenile fiction. 3. Beaches—Juvenile fiction.
[1. Tyrannosaurus rex—Fiction. 2. Dinosaurs—Fiction. 3. Beaches—Fiction.] I. Title.
PZ7.I217Se 2015 [E]—dc23 2014028637

Manufactured in China

1 3 5 7 9 10 8 6 4 2

Book design by Nancy Brennan Set in F Caslon Twelve
The illustrations for this book were created with Prismacolor pencils on vellum finish Bristol.

LIFEGUAR
OFF
DUTY